School for Dragons

"I only blow flames when I get excited," the little dragon whispered. "And I am going to try never to let excitement get the better of me."

"And just in case M1 *does* get excited," added Mr Wilkinson quickly, "I have installed two fire extinguishers in every room in the school. So I don't think we have anything to worry about. Isn't that right, M1?"

The dragon nodded vigorously.

"Now I want you all to be very welcoming and helpful to our first dragon pupil and enjoy being different from every other school in the world."

More *brilliant* Young Hippo School stories:

Off to School
Jean Chapman

The Grott Street Gang
Terry Deary

Nightingale News
Odette Elliott

Pet Swapping Day
Whizz Bang and the Crocodile Room
Susan Gates

Class Four's Wild Week
Malcolm Yorke

Or dare you try a Young Hippo Spooky?

Ghost Dog
Eleanor Allen

The Screaming Demon Ghostie
Jean Chapman

The Ghost of Able Mabel
Penny Dolan

The Green Hand
Tessa Krailing

Smoke Cat
Linda Newbery

Bumps in the Night
Frank Rodgers

The Kings' Castle
Ann Ruffell

Scarem's House
Malcolm Yorke

Ann Jungman

School for Dragons

Illustrated by John Eastwood

Hippo

To Darcy with love

Scholastic Children's Books,
Commonwealth House, 1-19 New Oxford Street,
London WC1A 1NU, UK
a division of Scholastic Ltd
London ~ New York ~ Toronto ~ Sydney ~ Auckland

Published in the UK by Scholastic Ltd, 1997

Text copyright © Ann Jungman, 1997
Illustrations copyright © John Eastwood, 1997

ISBN 0 590 19415 1

Typeset by Backup Creative Services, Dorset
Printed by Cox & Wyman Ltd, Reading, Berks.

10 9 8 7 6 5 4

Chapter 1

The Fire

Class 4J were spending the last twenty minutes of Thursday afternoon the way they spent the last twenty minutes of every afternoon. Mrs Jeffries was reading to them. No one could read a book like Mrs Jeffries – she had a different voice for every character and whenever there was a bit of suspense her voice went quiet and you could hear a pin drop.

On the particular Thursday afternoon when our story begins, Mrs Jeffries was reading her class *The Lion, the Witch and the Wardrobe* and they

had just got to the part where Aslan is tied down on the Stone Table. The children were staring at Mrs Jeffries, their eyes bright with interest and some with a tear beginning to well up, as they thought of the noble lion in the power of the White Witch. Then the firebell went.

"Oh, no!" groaned the children. "Do we have to go?"

"Yes, of course you do," said Mrs Jeffries briskly, grabbing the register with one hand and her whistle with the other. "Now quickly line up at the door as fast as you can. Darren, just *leave* everything and line up. Right, now, out into the playground through the hall door."

"What a dozy time to have a fire drill," moaned Lisa. "Just when the story was getting really interesting."

"I know," agreed Jessie. "I mean, I've seen the story on television and I know what's going to happen, but I was really enjoying it anyway."

"What does happen?" asked Nelson eagerly. "I've never seen the TV version. Does the wicked witch really kill Aslan?"

By then they were out in the playground and lining up with the rest of the school. Mrs Jeffries blew her whistle and then started to take the register in an irritated way.

"She thinks it's a silly time to have a fire drill too," Lisa whispered to Jessie, who nodded vigorously.

Suddenly someone called out: "Look! Look at the stockroom – there really *is* a fire!"

The whole school turned and looked at the hut near the kitchen, and there, sure enough, smoke was pouring out of the window. Inside they could see a few red and purple flames.

Just then the sounds of three fire engines could be heard, swooping down on the school. Mr Wilkinson, the headteacher, stood in front of all the children.

"All right everyone, that was great. You all walked out very sensibly. I'm proud of you. We don't think the fire is in any danger of spreading to the school but better safe than sorry. Now is everyone's register complete?" he asked the teachers. "No one's been burned to a cinder?"

All the children laughed as the teachers told the head that everyone was present and correct.

"Right," said Mr Wilkinson. "I want everyone to stand up against the far fence to make way for the fire engines. Off you go now, quickly!"

Once the children were all safely out of the way, the fire engines sailed into the playground, alarm lights flashing and bells ringing. The firemen leapt down and within seconds were spraying the stockroom with great blasts of water.

One of the firemen went up to Mr Wilkinson. "Any idea what might have started the fire, sir?"

"None at all – it's a complete mystery. In fact, now I come to think of it, no one has asked me for the key to the stockroom today. No, I just can't imagine how this happened."

It only took the fire brigade five minutes to put the fire out, and all the children cheered as the firemen took a bow. One of the firemen climbed in through the broken window and then shouted out in a loud voice, "He's in here, I've got the culprit. Stand back everyone, I'm bringing him out!"

The whole school strained to see the criminal who had started the fire.

"It must be a tramp who lit a cigarette," whispered Lisa.

"Or one of those people who start fires all the time."

"An arsonist," contributed Nelson.

"Yes, that's what I meant, one of them."

But when the fireman came out he was holding a small creature in his

arms. The creature had his head buried in the fireman's shoulder.

"It's a dragon!" said the fireman in an amazed tone. "It's a little dragon, and he started the fire!"

Chapter 2

M1

The whole school stared at the fireman and the bundle in his arms with utter amazement. Mr Wilkinson was the first one to find his tongue.

"All right everyone, now the fire's over and we know what caused it, we can all relax. I bet none of you thought it was a dragon – I certainly didn't. You all behaved very sensibly in the crisis; well done. It's about two minutes to home time, so will you get into lines in front of your teachers? Good. Now lead on, back into your classrooms, get your bags and coats and by then the bell should have gone."

"What do you think is going to happen to the dragon?" whispered Jessie, as they got into line again.

"The police will come and take him away, I suppose," answered Lisa.

"We don't know anything about it," Nelson pointed out. "We don't even know if it *is* a he. It might be a lady dragon."

"Whichever sex it is, it must be a baby dragon," commented Lisa. "I mean, it was so little the fireman could carry it out."

"All right, children, lead on," said Mrs Jeffries, and they began to walk back to the classroom.

"I'm not going home until I know what happened to that little dragon," said Jessie.

"Me neither," agreed Lisa.

"Are you two going to play after school?" asked Nelson.

"Yes," the two girls told him.

At that moment the bell rang.

"Put your chairs on the tables please," Mrs Jeffries told them. "Now off you go and let's hope that tomorrow isn't quite such an exciting day. Good afternoon, everyone."

"Good afternoon, Mrs Jeffries; good afternoon, everyone," chorused the children and they ran out talking about the fire and the dragon.

Lisa, Jessie and Nelson hung back. "Please, Mrs Jeffries, can we tidy up the classroom?"

Their teacher smiled at them. "Just dying to know about the dragon, aren't you?"

"Yes, Mrs Jeffries," they confessed.

"Well, why don't you pick everything up off the floor, make sure all the books are in tidy piles and that all the pencils are sharpened? Then come to the staffroom and I'll tell you what's happening with the dragon."

So the three children raced around the classroom, picking up every bit of rubbish on the floor and chucking it in the rubbish bin. Then Lisa stacked the books tidily, while Nelson tidied the book corner and Jessie sharpened the pencils.

"We've finished!" shouted Nelson. "Come on, let's go and tell Mrs Jeffries."

The three children raced as fast as they could down the stairs, through the hall and along the corridor. They stood outside the staffroom door and heard a lot of talk, and someone crying loudly.

"You knock," whispered Nelson.

"No, you," said Lisa.

"I'll do it," interrupted Jessie, and she knocked twice.

Mr Wilkinson opened the door. Looking past him the three children saw the dragon sitting on Mrs Jeffries' knee, weeping miserably.

"I didn't mean to start a fire," sobbed the dragon. "Really I didn't."

"Then what were you doing in the stockroom?" asked Mrs Jeffries gently.

The dragon gulped a few times, then blew his nose on Mrs Jeffries' hankie and said, "I wanted to look at the picture books."

There was a stunned silence.

"But you could do that at a library, couldn't you?" asked Mr Wilkinson.

"No, I couldn't," wept the dragon. "They don't want dragons in libraries, they're frightened we'll start a fire. So there isn't anywhere for me to look at books."

At that moment Mr Wilkinson remembered that Jessie, Nelson and Lisa were there. "What can I do for you three?" he asked.

"We wanted to tell Mrs Jeffries that we've finished tidying up the classroom."

"All right, very good," said the head. "I'm sure she heard you, so you can go off home now."

"No!" cried Mrs Jeffries. "These are

three of my best readers and I think they may be able to help us."

So the three children went into the staffroom and looked curiously at the little dragon. They decided it looked very small and sad, and not at all frightening.

"So you like looking at books, do you?" Mrs Jeffries asked the dragon.

"Oh, yes," replied the dragon, cheering up a bit. "I really do, better than anything."

"And can you read?"

"Oh, no," said the dragon, shaking his head sadly. "My dad says that dragons don't need to know how to read or learn any of the things that go on in a school, but I would so love to learn." And another tear ran down his nose.

Mrs Jeffries gave the dragon a hug, and kissed the top of his head. "Now here are my friends Nelson, Jessie and Lisa – they're all in my class and they are good readers. Maybe, if you ask nicely, they'd be willing to read to you."

"Oh, yes!" cried all three children at once.

"I'd love to," added Lisa.

"So would I," agreed Jessie.

"Cool!" said Nelson.

"But you'd have to promise not to burn us or anything," said Lisa.

"Oh, I wouldn't," said the dragon. "I only started the fire in the stockroom because I got so excited about the pictures in the book that I forgot."

"Do you think you can manage not to get too excited?" asked Mrs Jeffries.

"Oh, yes," the dragon assured her. "If I keep saying to myself 'no flames, no flames' it's all right, nothing but a bit of smoke now and again."

"Then we would love to read to you," agreed the children.

"Well, now that we've settled things, what are we going to do about getting you home, young man – I mean, young dragon?" demanded Mr Wilkinson.

"I can find my own way back, sir," said the dragon.

"Good," said Mr Wilkinson. "But I want your word that you won't creep into the stockroom again to read and start another fire."

"Oh, I won't, I promise I won't," said the dragon, shaking his head. "Oh, no, I'll never do that again. And thank you for not calling the police, my dad would have been very angry. May I go now?"

"Of course," said Mr Wilkinson. "And there are a few old books here that we were going to throw away. Would you like them?"

"Books for me?" The dragon's eyes lit up. "Books that I can take home for my very own? Oh, thank you, thank you. You are very, very kind. Oh, thank you," and he grabbed the books.

"We'll take you as far as the school gates," said Nelson.

"Yes," agreed Lisa. "And then we can make a date to read to you."

As they walked towards the gate the dragon began to look through his books. "They look very good. I can't wait to get them home."

"Would you like to know what they're called?" asked Lisa.

"We could tell you all that kind of thing," added Nelson eagerly.

"Do you have a name?" asked Lisa.

"It feels a bit odd calling you 'little dragon'. Do dragons have names?"

"Oh, yes," the little dragon assured them. "They most certainly do. My name is M1."

"M1!" cried the children in disbelief. "But that's the name of a road."

"Is it?" said the dragon. "Well, it's my name too. I'm the eldest boy child, you see. M for male, 1 for eldest."

"So what are your sisters called?" enquired Jessie.

"Well, there's Fl, F2 and F3. F for female. My brothers are called M2 and M3."

"Oh," said the children, a bit stumped for words.

"Well, I'll take the books and be gone then," smiled the dragon.

"No, don't go till we've made an arrangement to read to you," cried Nelson.

"It'll have to be after school," chimed in Jessie.

"Be here at four o'clock tomorrow," said Lisa. "By that time all the other children will have gone. We'll talk to Mrs Jeffries tomorrow about where to go. She'll help."

"Yes," agreed Nelson. "She always knows what to do."

The dragon beamed at them and said, "See you tomorrow then."

"See you tomorrow," the children called after him. "Bye, M1."

Chapter 3

Reading

The next day the three children could hardly wait for four o'clock.

"Do you think M1 will really turn up?" asked Lisa.

"Of course he will," retorted Nelson. "I mean, he's dead keen to know what's in all those books Mr Wilkinson gave him."

At break time Mrs Jeffries was on playground duty. The three children went up to her.

"Please miss, M1 wants us to read him some stories."

"Yes, and we arranged to meet M1 here at school, at four o'clock this afternoon."

"And we told M1 that you would let us go somewhere quiet to do it," concluded Jessie.

"Now just a minute, you three," said Mrs Jeffries. "What's all this about the M1 motorway?"

"Not the M1 motorway, miss. M1, the little dragon who started the fire."

"What an odd name," said Mrs Jeffries, frowning.

"It's because he's the first male

child," Nelson told her. "M is for male and 1 is for first. His brothers are called M2 and M3."

"Yes, and his sisters are called Fl, F2 and F3," added Lisa.

Mrs Jeffries laughed. "Oh, well, at least dragons don't have any arguments about what to call their children."

"But Miss, *can* we read to him?" asked Nelson anxiously. "We did promise and he seemed really enthusiastic."

"You've twisted my arm. All right, bring him to the classroom, and I'll stay late and tidy up while you lot read to him."

That afternoon, as soon as school finished, the children went and hovered around the school gate, waiting for the dragon. At ten past four he still wasn't there.

"He's not coming," said Jessie sadly.

"It's really odd because he was dying to hear the stories," frowned Lisa.

"Look!" cried Nelson. "Look behind that tree over there."

All three children looked, and sure enough there was a small puff of smoke rising up into the air. All three ran over to the tree and there stood the dragon, carrying all the books he'd been given the previous day.

"Hello, M1," said Nelson. "We've been waiting for you."

"What are you doing behind the tree?" asked Jessie.

"I didn't dare go into the school," whispered the dragon. "My dad says that I shouldn't have gone into the school yesterday and that schools are for children and not dragons and that the teachers wouldn't let me in after the fire. So I wasn't sure that you meant what you said yesterday."

"Of course we did," said Nelson.

"Yes, and Mrs Jeffries is staying late, so that we can read to you in the classroom," added Lisa.

The dragon grinned from ear to ear.

"Oh, thank you," he said. "Thank you very, very much."

So the four of them went into the classroom and the children took it in turns to read to the dragon. M1 listened intently to every word, laughing loudly at all the jokes, and biting his paws during the exciting bits. By 5.30 the children had read him three stories each.

"Time to go home, you four," said Mrs Jeffries.

"Just one more story, oh, please, please, please," begged M1.

"Well, all right," agreed the teacher. "But this definitely has to be the last one."

Every day on the dot of four o'clock M1 turned up to be read to. But now the summer holidays were coming and neither Mrs Jeffries nor the children were sure what to do.

"I think M1 should learn to read," declared Mrs Jeffries. "I mean, we can't always be here to read to him. I think M1 should come to school."

"What, *this* school?" asked the three children in amazement.

"And why not?" replied their teacher. "He's just as keen to learn as any of you."

So that afternoon when M1 turned up, the children asked him if he'd like to come to school and learn to read. The little dragon's eyes shone for a moment and then filled with tears. "Oh, I'd love to, it would be a dream come true; but my dad would never let me. My dad doesn't believe in education for dragons."

"Would you ask your dad to come and see me, M1? Then I'll see if I can persuade him to let you come to school," said Mrs Jeffries.

"I'll try," agreed the little dragon. "But I don't think he'll listen. He has very strong views, my dad, he really does."

The next day a very big, fierce-
looking dragon turned up with M1.

"My boy here says you want to see me," boomed Mr Dragon. "Some nonsense about teaching him to read. I hope he hasn't been bothering you or getting up to any mischief. You just tell me if he's out of order and I'll soon sort him out."

M1 stood by his father looking very worried.

"Oh, no, on the contrary, he has been coming to school every afternoon so that we can read him stories."

"Stories!" exclaimed Mr Dragon. "Waste of time, stories, if you ask me. Stories never did anyone any good. We don't have stories in our house, and a good thing too."

"Oh, I don't agree!" said Mrs Jeffries firmly. "Stories are the spice of life.

Now, what I wanted to say to you was that M1 seems very keen to learn to read and I would love to teach him. If I could persuade the headteacher to take him on, would you let M1 come to school?"

"School?" shouted Mr Dragon. "*School!* Whoever heard of a dragon going to school? No child of mine is going to get mixed up with all this education lark, and that's that."

M1 looked very miserable. Nelson looked at him and thought fast.

"That's a shame," he said. "Because every night I read to my brothers and sisters. My mum always says she doesn't know how she'd cope if I wasn't there to read them all a goodnight story. I've got five younger brothers and sisters just like M1. If M1 could read he'd be no end of a help to Mrs Dragon."

M1 grinned at Nelson. "It would be great, Dad. You know how cross you get when you get home from work and all the little ones are making a noise and rampaging. I could take them all upstairs and read to them."

"Yes," agreed Jessie. "And you could eat your dinner in peace and quiet."

"And you could sit by the fire and have a nice peaceful smoke of your pipe," added Lisa.

"I don't smoke a pipe," grumbled Mr Dragon. "Dragons don't need to. Still, it would be nice to come home to a quiet house."

"And you and Mrs Dragon could discuss what you've been doing during the day," added Mrs Jeffries. "And have a peaceful cup of tea together."

"Oh, do say 'yes', Mr Dragon," begged Lisa. "We all like M1 so much."

"Please, Dad," added M1 nervously. "I would really love to be able to read."

"Oh, I suppose so," groaned Mr Dragon. "I'm beginning to see that this reading lark has a good side to it. You can go to school, son, for one term, and then I'll have to review the situation. You'll be the first dragon ever to go to school; we'll have to see how it goes. What your grandfathers would say I hate to think. They'll be turning in their graves I shouldn't wonder."

M1 jumped up and down with delight and then gave his father a big hug.

"I'll talk to Mr Wilkinson tomorrow," said Mrs Jeffries. "And hopefully, at the beginning of next term our very first dragon pupil will join the school."

Chapter 4

Problems

Of course Mr Wilkinson did agree to let M1 join the school. "Any young creature who is as keen to learn as M1 is very welcome in my school," he declared. "So, M1, I expect to see you on the first day of next term and I hope your enthusiasm proves to be infectious."

On the first day of the new term M1 turned up in uniform – blue jeans and a T-shirt with the "Merringham Juniors" logo on it. Lisa, Nelson and Jessie ran over to him.

"You just stick with us," they told him. "You'll soon get the hang of it."

Some of the children ran up to them, calling, "Isn't that the dragon that started the fire in the stockroom?"

M1 looked upset. "I didn't mean to, really I didn't," he told them.

At that moment the whistle blew and the children went into the hall for assembly.

Mr Wilkinson welcomed them all back and made a few jokes. Then he told the school that they had a new pupil, a pupil with a difference. "Stand up M1, and come up here beside me," he said.

Treading gingerly, M1 made his way through the children to the headteacher.

"Now, children, this is M1. Most of you will remember M1 from the

time he accidentally set fire to the stockroom. M1, I want you to tell all the children here just why you did that."

M1 looked at his feet. "I wanted to look at all the pictures in the books."

"And now tell the children why it is you want to come to school."

M1 managed a small smile.

"Because I want to learn to read, more than anything in the whole wide world."

A murmur of surprise went through the hall.

"So put your hands up everyone who is going to help M1," said Mr Wilkinson.

Every hand in the hall shot up. M1 beamed at them all.

"Good," said the headteacher. "Now, M1, I want you to tell us all about yourself and your family, and why you're called M1, and why you're not dangerous."

So, blushing and shifting from one leg to the other, M1 told the children about his family.

"There are eight in my family – six children and my mum and dad, Mr and Mrs Dragon. I am called M1 because I am the first son – M for male and 1 for first. My mum and dad don't believe in education for dragons so I am the very first dragon in the whole world to ever come to a school."

Mrs Williams, the deputy head, put her hand up. "M1, I confess that I am a bit worried in case there's another

fire. I wonder if you could put my mind at rest on this matter."

M1 looked tearful. "I only blow flames when I get excited," he whispered. "And I am going to try never to let excitement get the better of me."

"And just in case M1 *does* get excited," added Mr Wilkinson quickly, "I have installed two fire extinguishers in every room in the school, including the stockroom, just in case of an unexpected emergency. So I don't think we have anything to worry about. Isn't that right, M1?"

The dragon nodded vigorously.

"Now I want you all to be very welcoming and helpful to our first dragon pupil and enjoy being different from every other school in the world."

Back in the classroom, M1 sat at the same table as Lisa, Nelson and Jessie. They promised Mrs Jeffries and the other children that if ever M1 did get excited they would grab the nearest

fire extinguisher. On the first day M1 put on an apron and began to paint a picture, something he had never done before. M1 loved covering the paper with brightly-coloured paint. When he had finished he stood back and looked at his work.

"Isn't it wonderful?" he exclaimed, jumping up and down. "Just look at that – my first painting in the whole world. I can't wait to show it to my mum and dad and M2 and M3 and Fl, F2 and F3."

A little flame darted out of his left nostril.

"Fire!" yelled Lisa and all the children picked up their jars and doused M1 with the dirty-coloured water.

M1 looked completely bewildered and then giggled. "I got excited, didn't I?"

"You certainly did," agreed Mrs Jeffries. "Now come on, M1, we'll go to the staffroom and find you a spare school uniform. You must take yours home to be washed."

After that everything went smoothly. M1 learned to read incredibly fast and after a few weeks he had almost caught up with Lisa, Jessie and Nelson. Every day M1 got a gold star for reading and went home with at least two books in his rucksack. When he wasn't playing with his friends, he would sit in the book corner buried in a book.

"If only all our children were like M1," sighed Mr Wilkinson. "Hard working, enthusiastic, helpful and polite. Maybe I should open a school for dragons."

There were a few more little fiery problems. One day in the playground M1 was skipping with some of the girls and having lots of fun turning the rope and singing:

"Jelly on a plate,
Jelly on a plate,
Wibble wobble, wibble wobble,
Jelly on a plate."

Unfortunately, as the pace quickened and the girls ran into the rope faster and faster, M1 started laughing and blowing fire. The rope caught alight.

In a flash the teacher on duty rushed across and threw her coat over the flames and M1, and rolled over on top of them. In a few moments the fire was out and M1 peeped out of the teacher's coat, coughing and gasping.

"Sorry, M1," said the teacher. "I hope I didn't crush you, but I had to put the flames out."

"I'm all right," wheezed M1. "I don't know what happened."

"You must have got excited," the teacher told him.

"Sorry," mumbled M1. "I didn't mean to."

After that there were hardly any more fires and M1 began to win every prize in the school for good work.

"Well," said Mr Wilkinson at a staff meeting. "We seem to have absorbed young M1 painlessly into our school; I don't see any problems ahead."

But Mr Wilkinson was wrong. For the very next day he got a letter saying that an inspector was coming into the school to look at the children's written work and use of language.

"An inspector," groaned the head-teacher to Mrs Jeffries. "Just as everything was going so nicely."

"Let any number of inspectors come!" declared Mrs Jeffries. "This is an excellent school, and we've got nothing to hide."

"I don't know about that," sighed Mr Wilkinson. "We've got M1 to hide for a kick-off!"

Chapter 5

The Inspector

On the day of the inspection the children all sat in neat rows in the hall, waiting for assembly to begin. M1 sat in between Nelson and Lisa. Mr Wilkinson came in with a woman none of them had seen before.

"Good morning, children."

"Good morning, Mr Wilkinson,"

chorused the school. "Good morning, everyone."

"Children, this is Mrs Ford who has come to our school to do a mini inspection, making sure that we're doing everything just right in our written work and the way we talk.

Now, as you all know, we *do* do everything just right so we have absolutely nothing to worry about, isn't that right, children?"

"Yes, Mr Wilkinson," chorused the children.

"So I want you to just go about your business as usual and be as helpful as possible. Will you do that?"

"Yes, Mr Wilkinson," chorused the children again.

"Good. Now go quietly back to your classrooms, please. Mrs Jeffries, would your class like to go first?"

The class stood up and followed their teacher out of the hall. M1 caught the inspector's eye and smiled. The inspector froze in horror and grabbed the head's arm.

"What is *that*?" she whispered, shaking. "That creature there? It looks like a dragon!"

"Oh, yes," said Mr Wilkinson, nervously. "That's M1, and he is indeed a dragon. The family live locally and he wanted to come to school desperately. He's turned out to be our very best pupil."

"A dragon in a school? Mr Wilkinson, what *can* you be thinking of? He'll have to go! You'll have to send for his parents immediately and get them to take him away once and for all."

"Oh, no," said the head. "I couldn't send him away – it would destroy the poor little chap. He absolutely loves school."

As the children left the hall some of them overheard the conversation. The word spread throughout the school that the inspector wanted M1 to be expelled.

"Don't tell M1," they whispered to each other. "He doesn't know and if he did he might get upset."

"Expelled indeed! We'll see about that!" declared Mrs Jeffries and she got M1 to come and stand in front of the class.

"Now, children, I am going to get M1 to blow some very small flames and I want you to write about fire. All right, M1, start blowing, please."

So M1 stood in front of the class blowing small orange and red and yellow and purple flames.

"Now, children, who can give me some good words to describe the colour of the flames?"

"Deep scarlet," cried one.

"Imperial purple," said another.

"Rich blue," called someone else.

"Luminous pink," came another response.

"Brilliant orange," contributed another.

"Excellent," said Mrs Jeffries, writing them up on the board. "And now describe the movement of the flames."

"Darting, flickering, shimmering, sparkling," came the responses.

"Excellent again," said Mrs Jeffries, writing them on the board too. "Now how about some smoke, M1."

M1 began blowing smoke just as the head and Mrs Ford the inspector walked in through the door. They stood at the back and watched.

"Some good words to describe the smoke now, children, to go with all these lovely words about flames."

"Grey."

"Drifting."

"Wafting."

"Curling elegantly."

"Wispy, cloudlike, teasing, dancing," cried different children.

"Wonderful!" declared Mrs Jeffries. "Now, I want you all to write a poem about fire and smoke, using the words on the board and any others you can think of. You too, M1."

The inspector watched the class working away in total silence and walked around looking at the poems.

"This is all excellent work, I'm very impressed," she said, and then she picked up M1's book and read his poem:

"*Not to make flames,*
Is one of my aims.
But when I do,
They're red, orange and blue."

"M1 in particular writes most poetically. Well, well, this *is* an unexpected sort of morning."

When the bell went and the inspector went off for a coffee, Mrs Jeffries breathed a sigh of relief. "Well done, children," she said. "I'm proud of you."

After coffee the inspector went into another class, which had asked to borrow M1.

"This science lesson, children, is about fire," said the teacher. "Now M1 is going to breath some fire for us and you can come up one at a time and feel the heat from the flames – not too close of course. Then I want you to tell me what we use fire for."

Soon there was a list on the board.

1. To keep warm
2. To cook with
3. To sterilize.
4. To look at: a lovely big fire in a dark room.
5. To generate electricity.
6. To run steam engines
7. To light our way: candles lamps etc.

After that M1 helped the class boil water and test the temperature. Then he burned a bit of paper in front of the class and they discussed what happened to cause it to turn black and shrivel up into flakes. Then the teacher said, "Well, this *has* been an informative lesson, hasn't it? Now I want you all to tell me, one at a time, what you have learned this morning. Stacy, you start."

"You see how useful a school dragon is?" murmured the head, smiling, as he left the classroom with the inspector.

"I'm beginning to," said the inspector. "That class was having a most interesting discussion. I'm very impressed by their use of language."

That afternoon another class decided to put on a play and asked to borrow M1. All the school was invited to watch at the end of the day. Full of curiosity, the children trooped into the hall and sat down. At the back sat the teachers and the inspector. A boy came on to the stage carrying a sword and a shield with a big red cross on it.

"I am Saint George," he cried, "and this is my story. In a land far away there dwells a wicked dragon. This dragon eats fair maidens. I must go quickly to that land and kill this fiendish creature and rescue the fair maidens. Come with me on my journey."

Saint George jumped on a horse and rode off. He came to a royal palace where everyone was weeping and wailing, no one more loudly than the King and Queen.

"What's up?" asked Saint George.

"The dragon," wept the Queen.

"What is that evil animal doing now?" demanded the knight.

"Our daughter, the beautiful Marianne – he wants to eat her! At this minute she is chained to a rock near the sea."

"Why are you giving her to the brute?" asked Saint George.

"He will burn up the whole land if we do not," the King told him and began to cry again.

"Never!" cried Saint George, waving his sword in the air. "I will rescue the princess – no problem."

The royals left and Saint George galloped off until he came to the princess hanging on the rock. All around children dressed as waves were wishing and washing near her. Then M1 came on looking very fierce.

"That princess is for me," he told Saint George. "Go away, I'm going to eat her."

"Never!" cried the knight. "I have come to rescue her."

M1 growled and snarled, "Then I'll eat you too, you silly knight."

M1 and Saint George had a very realistic fight, with lots of smoke and sparks and sword-slashing. In the end M1 lay on the ground, pretending to be dead, and Saint George rescued the princess who agreed to marry him and live happily ever after.

"Hurray," yelled the children. Then M1 came on with some notes and began to read:

"On behalf of class 4W I would like to thank you for coming to watch our

play and for listening so quietly. I
would also like to point out that very
few dragons are as horrible as the one
that Saint George killed."

While the children clapped and cheered, the inspector turned to Mr Wilkinson and said, "I can see M1 is a great educational asset. I don't see how I could recommend that he be sent away – he really is such a delightful little chap and so enthusiastic. Yes, I think he should be allowed to stay in this school."

Chapter 6

The Nativity Play

Christmas came around and Mrs Jeffries was asked to put on the school nativity play. Mrs Jeffries gave everyone a part except M1.

"Isn't there a part for me?" the dragon asked sadly. "Even a very small part?"

"To be honest with you, M1, I'm not

at all sure what to do. You're by far the best reader in the class and you would be by far the best narrator."

M1's eyes shone with pleasure. "Oooh, I would love to be the narrator," he declared.

"I know," said Mrs Jeffries, "but I'd be constantly worrying in case you started a fire. With everyone on the stage acting and all the people in the audience, you might forget yourself and get excited. We can't risk a fire at an event like this. So I'm hoping you'll be my production assistant and help me backstage."

"Yes, all right," said M1, trying hard not to show his disappointment.

Jessie put her hand up. "Please, miss, it's not fair that M1 be left out. I mean, he was so brilliant in *Saint George and the Dragon*."

A murmur of agreement ran through the class.

"Miss, if I stood next to M1 right through the play with a bucket of water at the ready, could he be the narrator?" demanded Jessie.

"Don't you want to be in the play yourself, Jessie?"

"Not really, I hate acting. I like making the costumes and the scenery."

"Good," said the teacher. "Then Jessie can be the set designer and the wardrobe mistress and the fire-putter-outer, just in case M1 does get excited."

"Then can I read the Christmas story after all?" asked M1.

"Yes, M1, you certainly can."

M1 grinned from ear to ear. "I won't let you and the class down, Mrs Jeffries. I'll be the very best narrator you ever had."

Everyone worked very hard on the nativity play, making the set and the costumes and learning their lines. M1 read the story without a single mistake.

"Miss, we need a fire for the shepherds to sit round," Lisa pointed out one day. "Could the narrator come and be the fire for a minute?"

Mrs Jeffries laughed to herself. "Do you want to be the fire, M1?" she asked.

"Oooh, yes," said the dragon, and he put down the script and lay on the floor in the middle of the shepherds, gently blowing a few flames. Then Lisa (who was playing the Angel) came on and told them that Jesus had been born.

"You've all got to go to Bethlehem and tell him you're pleased he's here," she told them.

As the shepherds got up to go, M1 scrambled up and went back to the side of the stage to continue the story.

When the night of the play came, the school hall was packed with parents. Right at the back sat the dragon family; the caretaker stood nearby with a fire extinguisher in his hands. Mrs Dragon had bought a new hat and was sitting rather nervously clutching her handbag and keeping a careful eye on M2, M3, Fl, F2 and little F3, who was sitting on her knee sucking a dummy. The young dragons, all dressed up in their best clothes, sat on the edge of their seats with just a tiny amount of smoke sneaking out of their nostrils.

The play started and when it came to the scene with the shepherds, M1 ran on to the stage. Then he lay on his back and gently breathed out tiny flames. The shepherds sat there warming their hands and moaning

about the high taxes and the bad weather. When the Angel came to tell them to go and follow the star, Nelson suddenly said, "We've got nothing to take the baby Jesus, but I bet it's cold in that stable. Let's take him our lovely fire, he'll like that."

"Good idea," said the other shepherds and they picked M1 up and carried him off.

"No!" whispered Mrs Jeffries urgently. "That's not in the script!"

But no one took any notice.

The scene changed to the stable. M1 came back on as the narrator, continued reading the story, and then ran off again. Mary sat holding Jesus, with Joseph standing behind her. There were a few cows and angels in the background. They were surrounded by straw. The shepherds walked in.

"You can look at the baby if you like," said Mary.

"He's lovely," the shepherds told her.

"We didn't have anything to bring the baby," Nelson said. "We're just poor shepherds. Then we thought it might be cold in a stable so we brought you a fire."

"That was a good idea," said Joseph.

"I was just saying to Mary that it was very cold in here."

"Yes, well, you just be careful where you put it. Keep it well away from the straw and the cows. From what I hear there are some kings coming this way and they're used to having their palaces all nice and warm."

"Yes," agreed Joseph. "They'll be well pleased."

The audience all roared with laughter and Mrs Jeffries breathed a huge sigh of relief.

M1 scrambled up and told the story of the three kings and then raced back to be the fire again. Then the three kings came on to the carol *We Three Kings of Orient Are*, and the audience joined in. They knelt before the baby and gave their gifts of gold, frankincense and myrrh. Then the kings went over to the fire.

"We've come a long way," they said. "Do you mind if we warm ourselves up a bit?"

"No, help yourselves," said Mary graciously.

"Thanks," replied one of the kings. "I'm getting on a bit and my knees are aching something terrible and a bit of a warm-up would do me good." And they went over to M1 who was lying on his back breathing out a few tiny red, orange and blue flames, as the audience laughed again.

"I've never seen an audience enjoy a nativity play so much," Mr Wilkinson whispered to Mrs Jeffries.

"I know," she agreed. "The children are making it up as they go along and it's very good."

M1 did his last reading and then everyone joined in singing *Away in a Manger*, while the shepherds and the kings knelt before the baby Jesus.

When the play was over the audience clapped and cheered. The performers joined hands and took a bow. M1 noticed his family at the back and waved.

Mr Dragon beamed proudly. "That's my boy," he told the caretaker. "The one that did all the reading and was the fire that warmed the baby Jesus."

"He took to it like a natural," the caretaker told Mr and Mrs Dragon. "I reckon school suits dragons."

"Ummm," mumbled Mr Dragon. "Yes, well, maybe."

"How do you do, Mr and Mrs Dragon and M2, M3, Fl, F2 and F3?"

said Mr Wilkinson, coming over to them. "How nice to see you all here. Did you have a good time?"

"Oh, yes, thank you," chorused the little dragons. "And we would all like to come to your school, please, Mr Wilkinson."

"And I'd be happy to have you," Mr Wilkinson told them.

"Please, Daddy, please can we all go to school with M1?" begged the little dragons.

"I'll think about it," said Mr Dragon, smiling. "I really will."

"You may think about it as long as you please," interrupted Mrs Dragon. "But *my* mind is made up. These children get into no end of trouble at home all day. They're bored and they need something to do and this education seems a good thing to me."

Mr Dragon looked surprised. "I didn't know you felt that way, my love."

"Well, I do," his wife replied. "Ever since M1 went to school and has been able to read to us all, I've been thinking that all our children should be educated. I like it when M1 reads me stories, and you like it when he reads the paper out to you."

Mr Dragon gave an embarrassed cough and let out a huge flame. The caretaker pointed the fire extinguisher at him.

"Well, if you insist, my dear, I suppose I'll have to say yes."

All the little dragons jumped up and down and cried, "Thank you Mummy, thank you Daddy, thank you Mr Head-teacher, thank you M1, thank you everyone! We're going to go to school!"

Jessie, Lisa and Nelson shouted, "Hurray, M1 can stay and all the little dragons are coming to school!"

Then M1 joined in, too: "Our school's a school for dragons!"

The End